For Sue
—J. P. L.

For my snowflake sister, Kate
—L. D.

Atheneum
Books for Young Readers •
An imprint of Simon & Schuster Children's
Publishing Division • 1230 Avenue of the
Americas, New York, New York 10020 • Text copyright
© 2003 by J. Patrick Lewis • Illustrations copyright © 2003
by Lisa Desimini • All rights reserved, including the right of
reproduction in whole or in part in any form. • Book design by
Ann Bobco • The text for this book is set in Stone Informal. • The
illustrations for this book are rendered in paper collage. •
Manufactured in China • First Edition • 2 4 6 8 10 9 7 5 3 1 •
Library of Congress Cataloging-in-Publication Data • Lewis, J. Patrick.
• The snowflake sisters / J. Patrick Lewis; • illustrated by Lisa
Desimini. • p. cm. • "An Anne Schwartz book." • Summary: Two
snowflakes named Crystal and Ivory travel on Santa's sleigh and
make their way through the wintry sky until they become part
of a snowboy in Central Park. • ISBN 0-689-85029-8 •
[1. Snowflakes—Fiction. 2. Santa Claus—Fiction.
3. Stories in rhyme.] I. Desimini, Lisa, ill. II. Title.
• PZ8.3.L5855 Cr 2003 • [E]—dc21 •
2002006138

J. Patrick Lewis

The Snowflake Sisters

illustrated
by

Lisa
Desimini

An

Anne

Schwartz

Book

Atheneum Books for Young Readers

SYDNEY

LONDON

TORONTO

NEW YORK

SINGAPORE

Said Crystal Snowflake to her twin,

"Look at what a spin I'm in,

Feather-light and falling . . . whoa!"

Sighed her sister, Ivory, "Oh,

Let us snow then, you and I,

While we have wet winds to fly,

While the children come and go—

Tongues inviting us to snow."

The Snowflakes weren't identical—
One was large and one was small,
One wore fleece and one wore lace.

Both spun beautifully in space
Between their cousins Pearl and Gray
In cold that took their breath away.

Upon a cloud the sisters slept,

Until a mighty night wind swept

Them off with seven billion four

Hundred million, maybe more,

Snowflakes down the countryside!

"Listen, Ivory!" Crystal cried.
"What is that tin bell I hear
Jingling . . . like a chandelier?"

And out of nowhere air there came,

Like something in a picture frame,

White whiskers over cherry red.

Eight reindeer flew full speed ahead.

Crystal shouted, "Ivory, hey,

Let's tag along on Santa's sleigh!"

They roller-coastered down until,

Tiptoe on a windowsill,

The twins held tight and watched St. Nick

By moonbeam, lamp, and candlestick.

Santa found himself a chair,

Sipped the eggnog waiting there,

Then went to work, and soon a sea

Of presents climbed the Christmas tree.

Two dolls, a sweatshirt,
  skateboard, skis,
Official soccer ball, a squeeze-
Mouse for the cat,
  a paperback
Of *Charlotte's Web*
  fell from his sack.

As he unwrapped the cellophane
Around a foot-long candy cane,
He found the sugar cookie tin
And laughed, "I mustn't get too thin!"

"He's leaving!" Crystal cried. "Let's go!"

The sisters *swooooshed* in swirling snow

Until at last they softly lay

Against the railing of the sleigh.

But who could see a snowflake kid

As small as that? Oh, Santa did,

And said, "Let's light the sky, Miss C.!

Merry Christmas, Ivor-e e e e e e e e!"

Six days switched off,

Six nights turned on,

From dusk to twilight,

Dark to dawn.

The cold kept up,

Snow hurried down.

Twin sisters hovered on a town

So big it made the world seem small—

The skyscrapers stood cloudy tall.

They saw the Lady in the Sky.

erage
& P. Index of 500 Stocks
ssell 2000 Index
High
Close
Low
Weekly
2002

Crystal said, "I wonder why
Half a million people stare
At snowflakes drifting on Times Square."

"It's not at *us*. It's that big ball.
And look! It's just about to fall."
Ivory couldn't help but shout,
"The New Year's in, the Old Year's out!"
The sisters never had such fun
Spinning, spinning, till they spun . . .

Fifth Avenue—
Two very tiny points of view.

Watch out! Poor Ivory had to grab
A gust of wind—to miss a cab.

Wet snow blew under squishy feet—
Squashed on 42nd Street.

Now what were they supposed to do?

Be buried under someone's shoe?
Fat snowflakes should explore the sky,
And they were much too young to die.

"Tomorrow," Ivory said, "let's arc
Our way on up to Central Park."

And there they saw the frozen lad
Built by a schoolgirl and her dad.

Two walnut eyes, a nose of twig,
A baseball cap one size too big,
A mouth made from a candy store—

And look!—what handsome clothes he wore.

"Wait a minute, please don't go,"

He said to them. "Do you girls know

How lucky we are being snow?

Before you get a minute older,

Stay here . . .

        play here on my shoulder."

And so they played till it grew dark

Cool games just right for Central Park.

Along the sidewalk drifts and peaks,

They had a ball for weeks and weeks!

At last the twins stuck to the boy,

Who'd never known such twice-ice joy.

And there they went on Wintering . . .

Until the splendor-ender, Spring.

The Snowflakes, melting, shed a tear
As they began to disappear,
But Winter called out cold and clear,

"I'll bring you back again . . . next year!"